NURSE'S
Night Before Christmas

NURSE'S
Night Before Christmas

Written by David Davis
Illustrated by James Rice

PELICAN PUBLISHING COMPANY

Gretna 2003

To my children, Christen and Caleb, whom I love very much,
and also to the Four Star Critique Group in Fort Worth, Texas, who gave
me help, love, and support.

The word "Pelican" and the depiction of a pelican are trademarks
of Pelican Publishing Company, Inc., and are registered
in the U.S. Patent and Trademark Office.

Library of Congress Cataloging-in-Publication Data

Davis, David (David R.), 1948-
  Nurse's night before Christmas / written by David Davis ; illustrated
by James Rice.
     p. cm.
Summary: Santa Claus brings Christmas Eve surprises to the patients and
hard-working staff of Angel Hope General Hospital.
  ISBN 1-58980-152-0 (hard cover : alk. paper)
[1. Christmas—Fiction. 2. Hospitals—Fiction. 3. Santa Claus—Fiction.
4. Stories in rhyme.] I. Rice, James, ill. II. Title.
  PZ8.3.D2894Nu 2003
  [E]—dc21
                                            2003009282

Printed in China
Published by Pelican Publishing Company, Inc.
1000 Burmaster Street, Gretna, Louisiana 70053

NURSE'S NIGHT BEFORE CHRISTMAS

'Twas late Christmas Eve at Angel Hope General.
I was night-shift head nurse (with no shift deferential).

My stockings weren't hung at the nurse station there.
I'd been working twelve hours and had on my one pair.

My children were home asleep in their beds.
I had to be here to give holiday meds.

I worked the ER to help those waylaid.
It was hard to keep up, with just me and one aide.

Chart notes were hung on the wall with great care.
Our work load was heavy and break times were rare.

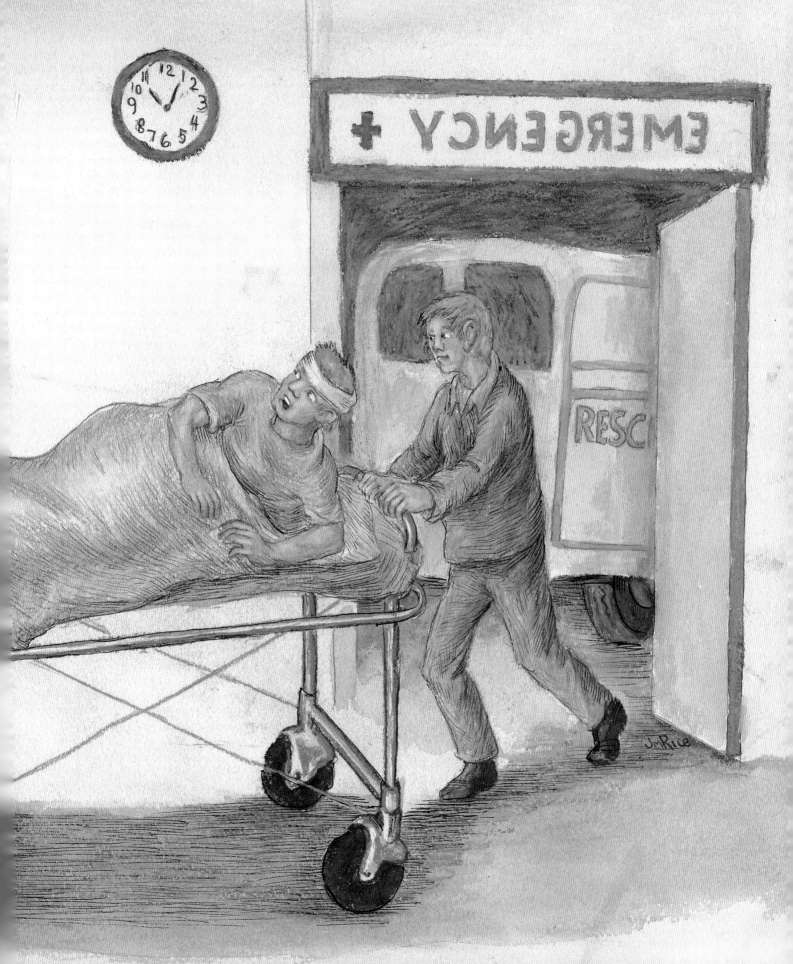

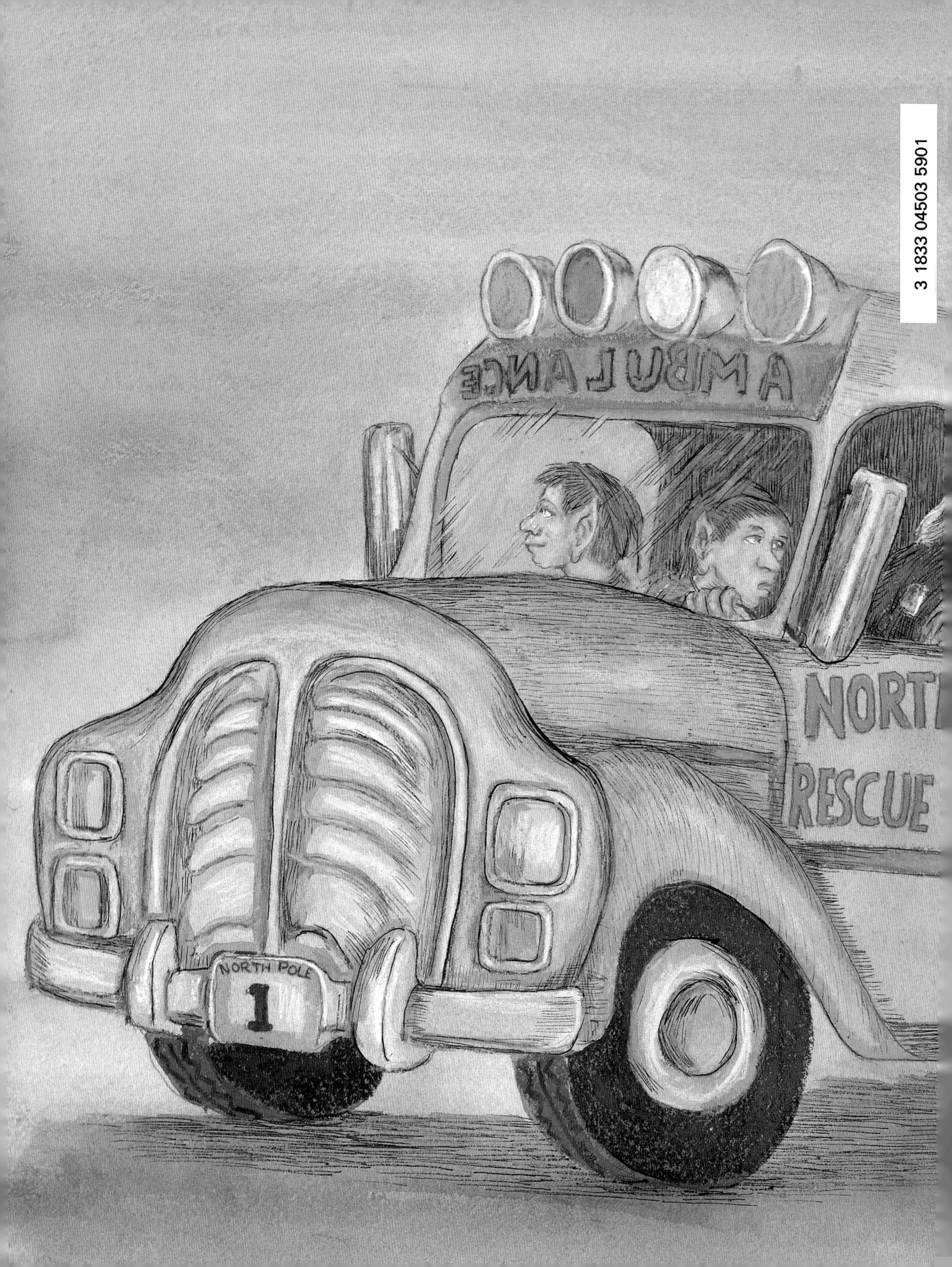
AMBULANCE
NORT
RESCUE
NORTH POLE
1

When outside the doors I heard such a din,
I called up the guard to see who'd backed in.

I stared out the door—it seemed like a dream—
And read the truck logo: "North Pole Rescue Team."

A surgical cap topped the driver's old head.
The ambulance lights flashed white, green, and red.

His face was all rosy from the snowfall outside.
The patients fell silent, and all stared wide-eyed.

They figured that something had commenced to be weird.
No doctor they knew had a long thick white beard!

He wore hospital scrubs and a long red lab coat.
And an elfin ward clerk jotted down all he spoke.

He knew which units to open and which units to close,
And his round granny glasses perched low on his nose.

"Don't worry, nurses. I know what to do!"
His smile was so bright, it made me grin too!

"Christmastime patients are just where I'm at.
We'll have holiday cheer around this ward *stat!*"

Up to my station raced eight R.N. elves.
They craved double shifts and begged for two twelves!

They showed their credentials and Christmas lab coats,
And on top of it all, they each offered to float!

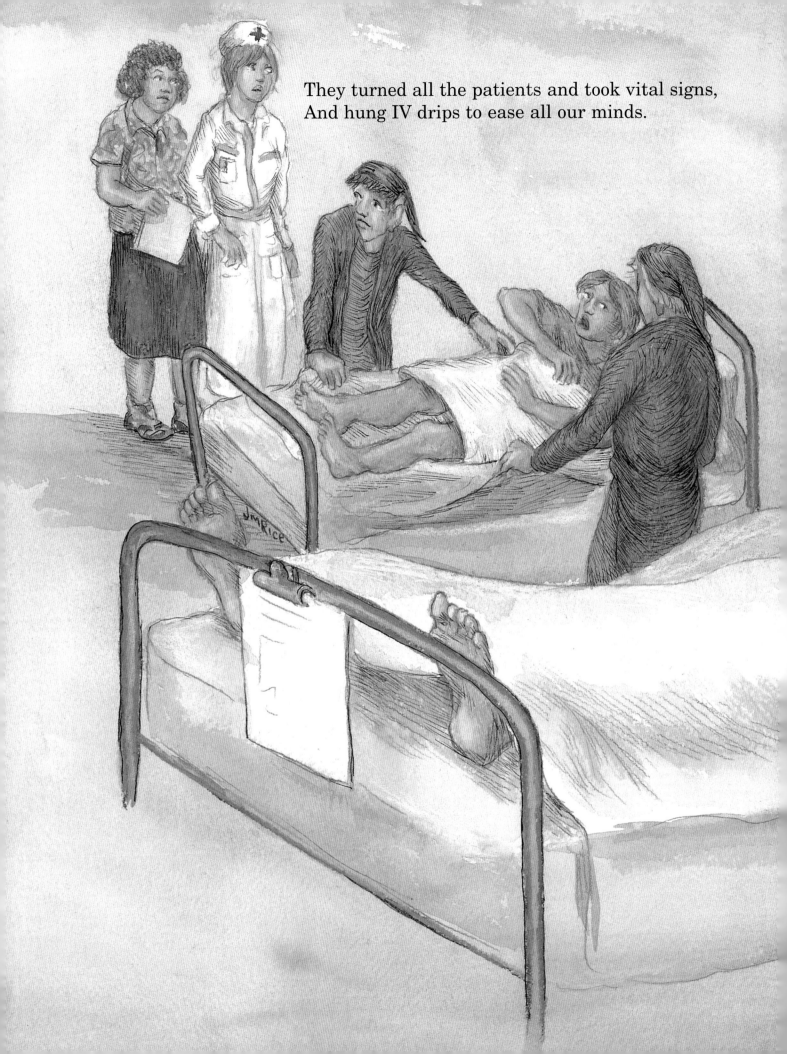

They turned all the patients and took vital signs,
And hung IV drips to ease all our minds.

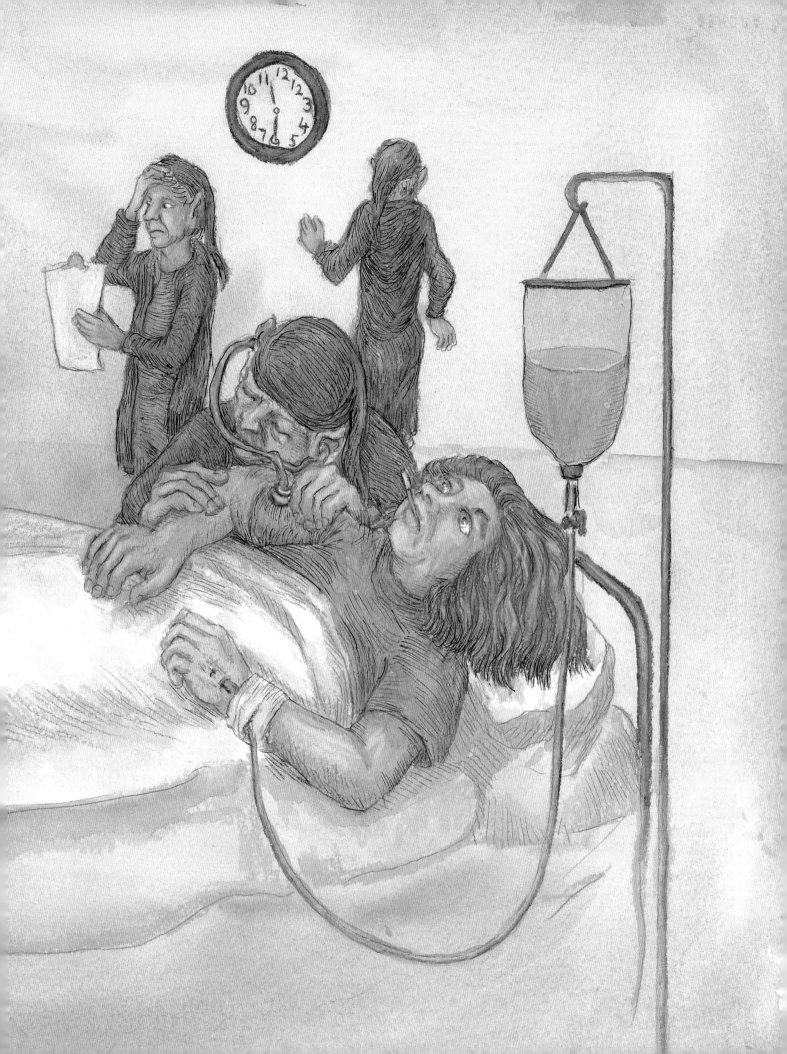

They emptied the bedpans and changed all the sheets,
Bathed all the patients, while we rested our feet.

In no time at all, the charts were all done.
Outpatients were seen and it was time for some fun.

I thought for a minute, "This must be a trick."
Now I could see it was Saint Emergency Nick!

Nick's holiday bag held toys for the kids.
Then he gave gifts to us that just flipped our lids!

There were crash carts with cakes and lots of fruit pies,
An espresso machine to help open our eyes.

He gave all the interns new pens for free
And pulled out some course books on humility.

I was surprised—there were no nurse egos here.
With a wink he explained, "For the heart surgeons, dear."

He brought me some shoes for my two aching feet
And a stethoscope plated with gold that was neat!

Next he used his benevolent gift for the gab
To end our longstanding feud with the lab.

Just when I thought he'd exhausted the loot,
He pulled bonus checks from inside his boot.

His eyes—how they twinkled, like two small blue blazes—
He'd jawboned the board—and they gave us all raises!

Nick brought in a tree for the waiting-room crowd.
It glowed with such warmth that it made us all proud.

His visitation was short; he let us all know.
He bowed from the waist and then turned to go.

Nick waved to us all as he jogged out the door.
"I've more consultations and house calls galore!"

He blinked and then added, "Good night, all my friends!"
And he smiled and exclaimed, "Merry Christmas—PRN!"